Clifford's
Class Trip

For Ace Hunter Burton
—N.B.

The author would like to thank Manny Campana and Grace Maccarone
for their contributions to this book.

Copyright © 2003, 2011 by Norman Bridwell

ISBN 978-0-545-22319-5

10 9   18/0

Printed in the U.S.A.   40
First printing, July 2003
This edition printing, January 2011

Clifford's
Class Trip

Norman Bridwell

SCHOLASTIC INC.

Emily Elizabeth's class is going
on a trip today. Clifford comes too.

Some girls and boys ride the bus.
Some ride Clifford.

They are ready to learn about
animals from the sea.

First they see seals.

A seal hits a ball.

Clifford hits it back.

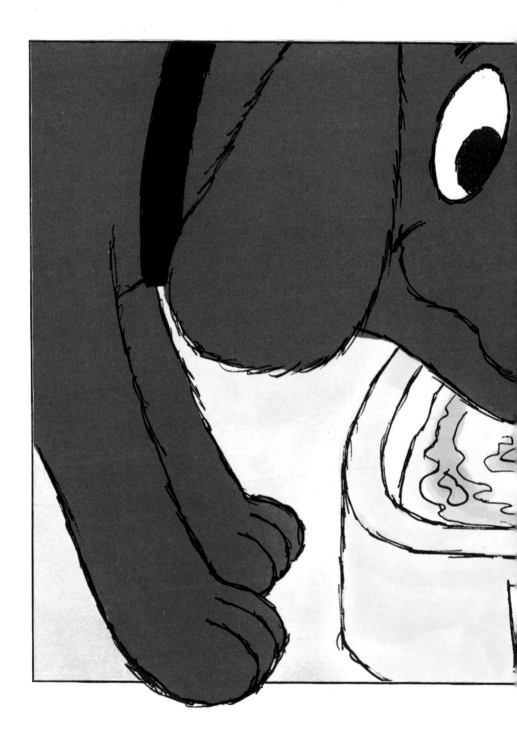

O NOT PUT HANDS
IN POOL!

They go to the next tank.

What is this?

Clifford wants to know.

Uh-oh! He gets too close.

A friend comes to help.

Clifford says thanks.

Then Clifford sees a baby whale.

The whale needs to go
back to the ocean.
But the truck won't start.

Can you guess who can help?

Clifford can!

Clifford carries the children
and the whale.

At the dock, they get on a boat.

Soon they are far out in the bay.

The little whale is home.

Big whales come to meet her.

And Clifford makes some
new friends!

It was the best class trip ever!